D E F G
K L M
Q R S T
X Y Z

For Jackie Kaiser, a true friend to both me and this book
—S.O.

For Mom
—J.G.

 Published in the United States by Random House Children's Books,
a division of Penguin Random House LLC, New York.
Published simultaneously in Canada by Tundra Books in 2018.

Library of Congress Cataloging-in-Publication Data is available upon request.

ISBN 978-1-5247-1331-7 (trade) — ISBN 978-1-5247-1332-4 (lib. bdg.) — ISBN 978-1-5247-1333-1 (ebook)

MANUFACTURED IN CHINA
10 9 8 7 6 5 4 3 2 1
First Edition

Owls Are Good at Keeping Secrets

An Unusual Alphabet

Words by
Sara O'Leary

Pictures by
Jacob Grant

Random House New York

Aa

Alligators think you'd like them
if you got to know them.

Bears sometimes want their mothers to kiss it better.

Chipmunks love to stay up past bedtime.

Dd

Dragons cry at happy endings.

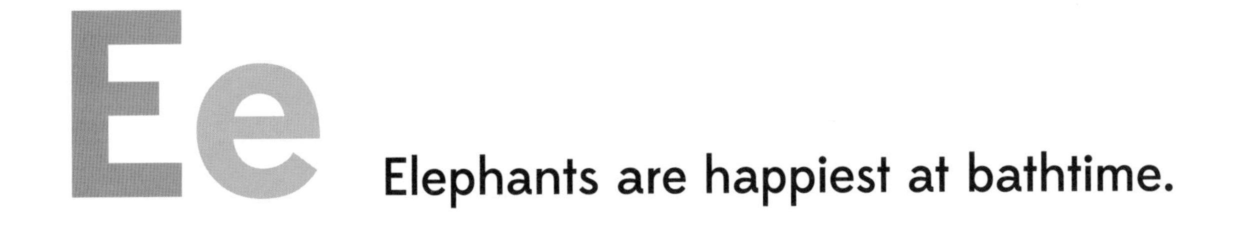

Ee

Elephants are happiest at bathtime.

Foxes always think you should
take one more picture.

Giraffes usually have just
one best friend.

Hh

Hedgehogs can't help being curious.

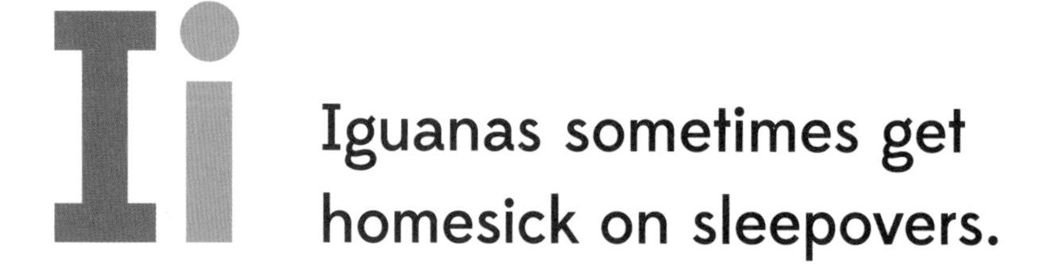

Ii

Iguanas sometimes get homesick on sleepovers.

Jellyfish don't care if you think they look funny when they dance.

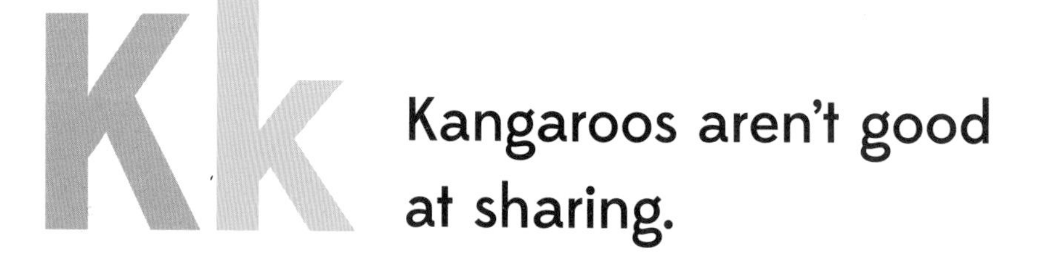

Kangaroos aren't good at sharing.

Ll

Lions like a nice nap.

Mm

Meerkats love a parade.

Nn

Narwhals can be perfectly happy all alone.

Owls are good at keeping secrets.

Pp

Penguins love a big family get-together.

Qq

Quail get quite tired of being told to be quiet.

Rr

Raccoons are always the first to arrive for a party.

Starfish can never tell when
other starfish are waving.

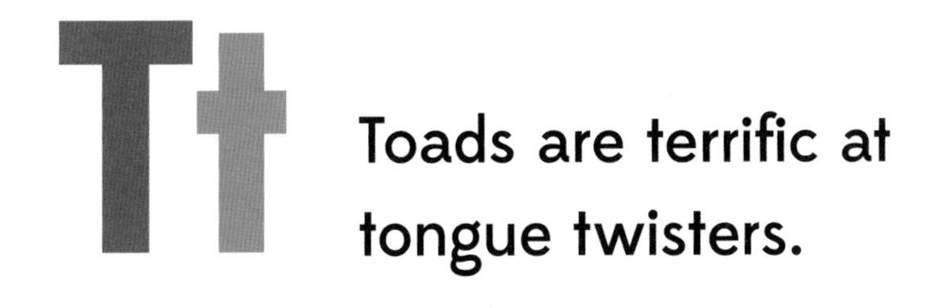

Toads are terrific at
tongue twisters.

Unicorns believe in themselves.

Voles always want just one more book.

Wolves don't like being told
to smile.

Xx

X-ray fish just can't help
looking cool.

Yy

Yaks giggle at their own jokes.

Zebras would like to be first.
Just once.

a b c
h i j
n o p
u v w